PRAISE FOR M. L. BUCHMAN

A fabulous soaring thriller.

— TAKE OVER AT MIDNIGHT, MIDWEST BOOK REVIEW

Meticulously researched, hard-hitting, and suspenseful.

— PURE HEAT, PUBLISHERS WEEKLY, STARRED REVIEW

Expert technical details abound, as do realistic military missions with superb imagery that will have readers feeling as if they are right there in the midst and on the edges of their seats.

— LIGHT UP THE NIGHT, RT REVIEWS, 4 1/2 STARS

Buchman has catapulted his way to the top tier of my favorite authors.

— FRESH FICTION

Nonstop action that will keep readers on the edge of their seats.

— Take Over at Midnight, Library Journal

M L. Buchman's ability to keep the reader right in the middle of the action is amazing.

— Long and Short Reviews

The only thing you'll ask yourself is, "When does the next one come out?"

— Wait Until Midnight, Romantic Times Book Reviews, 4 stars

The first...of (a) stellar, long-running (military) romantic suspense series.

— The Night is Mine, Booklist, The 20 Best Romantic Suspense Novels: Modern Masterpieces

I knew the books would be good, but I didn't realize how good.

— Night Stalkers series, Kirkus Reviews

Buchman mixes adrenalin-spiking battles and brusque military jargon with a sensitive approach.

— PUBLISHER's WEEKLY

CROSSING THE RIVER

A SCIENCE FICTION ROMANCE

M. L. BUCHMAN

Buchman Bookworks

SIGN UP FOR M. L. BUCHMAN'S NEWSLETTER TODAY

and receive:
Release News
Free Short Stories
a Free book

Get your free book today. Do it now.
free-book.mlbuchman.com

Other works by M. L. Buchman: *(* - also in audio)*

Thrillers

Dead Chef
Swap Out!
One Chef!
Two Chef!

Miranda Chase
*Drone**
*Thunderbolt**

Romantic Suspense

Delta Force
*Target Engaged**
*Heart Strike**
*Wild Justice**
*Midnight Trust**

Firehawks
MAIN FLIGHT
Pure Heat
Full Blaze
*Hot Point**
*Flash of Fire**
Wild Fire
SMOKEJUMPERS
*Wildfire at Dawn**
*Wildfire at Larch Creek**
*Wildfire on the Skagit**

The Night Stalkers
MAIN FLIGHT
The Night Is Mine
I Own the Dawn
Wait Until Dark
Take Over at Midnight
Light Up the Night
Bring On the Dusk
By Break of Day
AND THE NAVY
Christmas at Steel Beach
Christmas at Peleliu Cove

WHITE HOUSE HOLIDAY
*Daniel's Christmas**
*Frank's Independence Day**
*Peter's Christmas**
*Zachary's Christmas**
*Roy's Independence Day**
*Damien's Christmas**
5E
Target of the Heart
Target Lock on Love
Target of Mine
Target of One's Own

Shadow Force: Psi
*At the Slightest Sound**
*At the Quietest Word**

White House Protection Force
*Off the Leash**
*On Your Mark**
*In the Weeds**

Contemporary Romance

Eagle Cove
Return to Eagle Cove
Recipe for Eagle Cove
Longing for Eagle Cove
Keepsake for Eagle Cove

Henderson's Ranch
*Nathan's Big Sky**
*Big Sky, Loyal Heart**
*Big Sky Dog Whisperer**

Love Abroad
Heart of the Cotswolds: England
Path of Love: Cinque Terre, Italy

Other works by M. L. Buchman:

Contemporary Romance (cont)

Where Dreams
Where Dreams are Born
Where Dreams Reside
Where Dreams Are of Christmas
Where Dreams Unfold
Where Dreams Are Written

Science Fiction / Fantasy

Deities Anonymous
Cookbook from Hell: Reheated
Saviors 101

Single Titles
The Nara Reaction
Monk's Maze
the Me and Elsie Chronicles

Non-Fiction

Strategies for Success
Managing Your Inner Artist/Writer
*Estate Planning for Authors**
Character Voice
Narrate and Record Your Own
*Audiobook**

Short Story Series by M. L. Buchman:

Romantic Suspense

Delta Force
Delta Force

Firehawks
The Firehawks Lookouts
The Firehawks Hotshots
The Firebirds

The Night Stalkers
The Night Stalkers
The Night Stalkers 5E
The Night Stalkers CSAR
The Night Stalkers Wedding Stories

US Coast Guard
US Coast Guard

White House Protection Force
White House Protection Force

Contemporary Romance

Eagle Cove
Eagle Cove

Henderson's Ranch
Henderson's Ranch

Where Dreams
Where Dreams

Thrillers

Dead Chef
Dead Chef

Science Fiction / Fantasy

Deities Anonymous
Deities Anonymous

Other
The Future Night Stalkers
Single Titles

ABOUT THIS BOOK

***Persephone** loves the free-wheeling lifestyle of an inter-planetary freighter pilot. Like her namesake of Ancient Greece, she lives a two-fold life. Part of the year sequestered in deep space and part in various ports with a good friend and hopefully a willing man.*

*Until her heading converges with fellow pilot **Reggie**. Shy yet quirky, teasing yet kind. He possesses great depths that only Persephone can cross over.*

When their orbits suddenly diverge, Reggie must plot a new course to reclaim his one true love.

PROLOGUE

*H*ER FACE.

A hand painting her face.

An ochre overtone highlight for the cheeks.

But not for the deep-space dark of her hair.

At first, clean carbon seeking her outline. For a while, the artifice of sharp acrylics questing after her inner form. But now it is only oils—their muddy tang, smooth flow, and shading—that provide any hope of capturing her skin.

I am aware of her skin, the painting, and the tones.

However, the "I" is rather more elusive.

Once there was a name.

One so often spoken that there was no need to remember it, for it had lived on the tongue with an indescribable depth of meaning.

1

"No! You didn't!"

Persephone giggled. It was her most significant challenge to ever being dignified—she'd never learned to laugh, which left her with the delighted giggle from childhood as a sole mechanism for displaying humor.

Only the raucous cheering of the Tycho Tavern's crowd watching the vid of the Moonball championship game saved her from completely embarrassing herself. The Titans were up by two, but it was a knuckle-biting battle—if you were a Moonball fan.

"I just can't believe you," Melora toasted her with a pint of Aitken Dark, named for Luna's deepest crater which lay on Farside, near the South Pole. "He's so handsome and so rich," her friend groaned with envy.

For her, those were marks against him rather than in his favor.

Persephone preferred the white ale of Mare Frigoris, served mere degrees above freezing. If held on the tongue to warm, the effervescence expanded until it almost burned, but with a heat of a vaguely remembered bright winter's day. Her family had launched when she was eight and by ten she'd lost the musculature to ever return down Earth's gravity well and test her memory.

She also preferred her men that way: smooth, warm, and leaving little more impression than a long-ago adventure in the snow.

Her father had died in the Lift. The overused acceleration couch had collapsed at 10 g's and snapped his back along with it. They'd listened to him die, unable to rise from their own couches to help him. Her mother had hung on until Persephone was sixteen, but been a mere shadow of the woman she remembered on Earth. The day after Persephone had stepped into the Flight Academy, her mother had stepped out an airlock without a suit.

Yes, Persephone preferred her men at a distance.

Already half grown when she climbed the grav well, she didn't have the long structure of the space-born nor the squat tank-like stature of the New Earthers, instead landing uncomfortably between so that she belonged with neither group. A glance around the raucous bar identified only two others with builds similar to her own but neither looked as if it bothered them. Twenty years aloft and she still felt the divides as clearly as a flight path on her ship's nav console. Her naturally black hair was almost as rare now as Melora's blonde, perhaps why they'd been drawn together at first.

"I still can't believe that you stole Reggie's ship!" Melora's voice was loud enough she'd be announcing it to the crowd, if it weren't for the game.

Reggie. There was a man who failed to fit smooth, warm, or forgettable. For half a solar year she'd tried to shed him like any other, yet still found herself in his bed whenever they were in the same port.

"Where did you put it? Let me guess...Kepler Crater?" Melora had to practically shout over a sudden wave of groans as the Tycho Titans gave up a point to the Grimaldi Grinders. It was rising semi-finals and emotions were lashing loudly off the fused rock walls of the underground hole that was Tycho Tavern. It was a popular watering hole among the space pilots and crew and was always busy. But the game had packed it so tight, they'd barely kept their stools at the bar.

"Nope. Not Kepler."

"The Imbrium Yard?"

"You'll never guess. It's right here in Tycho, just not on any landing pad."

"You didn't!"

"I did! I parked it inside the Chinese megafreighter *Good Luck*—the one that collided with its own braking booster and dumped a half million tons of habitat parts on top of their base in Clavius. Utterly destroyed it and most of the Chinese space effort."

Melora held up a hand and she slapped it a high-five.

Persephone had made the salvage yard owner promise not to actually scrap Reggie's ship, but she didn't want to ruin a good story with practical details.

"What about his ship's locator beacon?" Of course, there was a reason she liked Melora—closest thing she had to a friend. Her mind worked much like Persephone's.

"Rigged a battery and slipped it under his own bunk at the Tycho hostel."

Melora's look said that she knew exactly how she'd gotten past his private security, but Reggie had so deserved it after he'd shafted her on the Martian contract. That was a lucrative run…or should have been. Guy was a worm. Worse, she'd known that *before* she'd started sleeping with him.

Except that wasn't right.

No, if he was a worm, she'd have ignored him. He was a touch ruthless—which was a lot like her. And went after what he wanted with an alarming directness— which had initially charmed her, but now was causing worry. Stealing and hiding his ship in a scrap yard was more her style and would hopefully sidetrack him until she was ready to lift for Jupiter space and—

"Inside the *Zhù nǐ hǎoyùn*. Wishing me *good luck*. That *was* creative!"

Melora nearly snorted in her beer as Reggie's deep voice sounded close behind them.

Twelve words. Well, ten if she counted the ship's name as one. Still, that was ten more than he typically spoke at any one time. Her ploy had really gotten to him.

Persephone managed to hide her smile in her beer. Any other man would have taken days to track down where she'd hidden his ship—and a whole lot never would. It had taken Reggie less than a day. Definitely not a worm.

———

THE COLOR OF HER LONG FLOW OF DARK HAIR REMAINED elusive. No shade captured it. Not sable or raven. Neither obsidian nor ebony. It would shimmer when she smiled as if, rather than being mortal hair stuff, it and she were forms constructed wholly of emotion.

Emotion.

A word with a definition but no meaning.

2

"I DID NOTHING TO HARM YOUR SHIP." IT HAD ONLY TAKEN A year together for his formidable reticence to allow complete sentences in her presence. He still clammed up around Melora and others; his reserve permeated down to his very bones.

"Except?" Persephone been upsystem for months, only to run into him at Europa's Launchpub. After an incredibly satisfying night together, Reggie had suited up and followed her out onto the base. He was clearly eager to personally witness his latest effort in their mutual near-destruction pact. Not that he would show it, of course, but she could tell.

Expecting it, she'd beefed up security on the *Cerberus* during the long and lonely nights of a space crossing. But that wouldn't stop a man of Reggie's caliber.

"At least as long as you're beside me, I know it won't be anything lethal," she teased.

"Not for more than one person, anyway. Perhaps the

question you should be asking is whether it is a death trap for the one who leads, or the one who follows?"

"Perhaps," Persephone was tickled that he spoke to her, for she knew how hard that was for him. Also that he, of all the men she'd ever known, had puzzled out how to charm her.

Men were never a challenge and only rarely of interest.

She'd dismissed Reggie Armstrong at first. The Armstrong lineage could prove no direct connection to the first astronaut to walk on the moon, but they might as well have. An old and powerful family, they did trace directly to the First Colony *Mayflower* launch. His family owned most of Tycho Station—which she supposed they deserved as they'd also built most of it.

But his arrogantly refined manners had slowly been revealed to be more just another expression of how deep down the inner man resided. At times she felt like a prospector seeking the bits of gold that time had taught her were always there.

She cycled the lock and jumped back, slamming into him. Nothing.

He held her for a moment longer than necessary to make sure she was steady. A major statement for him.

But there was something. A single flake of impossibly red color in the middle of the airlock floor. She moved forward and inspected it cautiously. It moved when she brushed it with her suit glove, but it was so thin she wasn't able to grab it.

It was tempting to cycle the outer door with Reggie still out on the gantry, but she let him join her. She didn't ask what the tiny bit of red was. Instead, she'd experience the adventure as it unfolded.

Even out of her pressure suit, she didn't recognize the object. It was so light that she couldn't feel it resting on her bare palm in Europa's one-eighth grav except as a breath-soft tickle. It was redder than a hull breach warning light—as if it was the definition of red.

Through the inner hatch, she found another red flake, placed two steps aft rather than toward the control room.

Another at her cabin door.

She'd have to figure out later how Reggie had gotten aboard her ship. Because unlike her stealing *his* ship's security on the Moon—by finagling a password for herself into his comp's master terminal after slipping out of his arms while he slept—he'd never been aboard her ship.

Which was curious. They'd been paired for a year now, at least whenever they were in a common port, yet they'd always slept aboard *his* ship or in a port facility. Didn't he have curiosity? Or was he honoring her privacy? At least until today.

"Pay off the port captain?" She asked, but couldn't stop herself from opening her cabin door to see what lay within.

"I'd—"

"Right, you'd never do anything so crass. Depending on someone else in order to commit your crime."

"My crime?" Almost a note of surprise. Almost.

"The crime of tresp..." she tapered off as she tried to make sense of what she was seeing. Her room was unchanged. Desk, chair, kick-down toilet and sink, and a double wide bunk. Not stowed in its normal acceleration-safe position. Instead down, with pillows fluffed.

And on the corner of the desk she used as a nightstand, a vase stood. From it sprang a single, brilliant red rose.

"I've seen images. But I've never..." She could only wave at it helplessly.

"They have a scent," Reggie whispered. "One that the holos don't capture."

She moved over and could feel the fragrance tickling the air before she was even close. A tentative sniff grew of its own accord to closing her eyes to block out all other sensory input. It smelled of a forgotten Earth and of a promise. A promise of...

Persephone turned slowly and opened her eyes to look at Reggie. Space-born tall. Darkly handsome. Venturing out of his shell only in her presence.

He regarded her with that perfect stillness that had so drawn her to poke at him. Reggie would never say what he was thinking or what he felt about anything. Instead, Reggie simply—was. Occasionally she'd accused him of being an android. At other times she'd recommended he get a cybernetic implant.

For what?

For an emotional response.

But while Reggie Armstrong might not be expressive, his actions spoke volumes. And this time it also asked a question. Many questions in one.

"Yes," she didn't need to think about it.

Reggie didn't need to ask what she was answering.

They both knew, and the future lay long and clear ahead of them.

––––––

THE RISE OF THE CHEEKBONES WAS OFF, BUT IT WASN'T.

It was correct.

The hair color was right, but...the lie was wrong.

That was it.

The onyx fall was always tucked behind the right ear.

Exposing the ear balanced the more abrupt curve of her high-grav cheekbone rather than the longer taper of the space-born.

The tip of the nose tugged down by the hint of a smile.

The lips...

3

"I've never been to a real wedding," Melora whispered in her ear.

"Nor I," Persephone could barely whisper back past the tightness in her throat. They were rare enough in modern society to be considered anachronistic— declaring a life bond so formally. Her practical side had always thought them silly. But an inner part of her, the part that only Reggie could reach, seemed to be deeply touched.

Reggie had arranged it all. Not with his family on the Moon, who didn't treat him well at all as far as Persephone was concerned.

He might be reserved to the extreme, but she could *feel* him. Even now, she could feel the infinite care he'd taken in somehow arranging interplanetary cargo schedules across seven corporate states so that her friends could all be in this place at this time. A small wedding, barely twenty, but they were here for her in this moment. And her future husband had done that for her.

When she'd asked who would stand for him, he answered with that shrug of his. "As long as you are there, nothing else matters."

It was a degree of kindness that she barely remembered from her parents and had seen so little of since. But it was as inherent in Reggie Armstrong as if programmed into his blood.

Blood, the color of the world around them. Not of heart's blood pumped out of a dying body, but the color of life. Bringing the heat she could feel so close beneath his skin when they made love. She could feel him burn for her and every time it made her burn for him.

She and Melora stood at the back of the glass cathedral (no lesser word could describe it) atop Olympus Mons—the tallest mountain on any planet in the solar system. Though they were over twenty kilometers into the atmosphere, they were practically standing outside. Fused from the soil's silica, the dome rose in great sheets of grandeur impossible under Earth's heavy grav and high winds. Olympus Mons even rose clear of the planet-girdling dust storms.

The stained-glass windows were worked, in shades of Martian iron red, directly into the glass walls. The images celebrated voyages: from the first feeble attempts of Sputnik and Mercury to the Pioneer probes still heading for the stars, and the manned Odyssey Colony missions that had long since left them behind.

"Adventure," Melora followed her gaze. "Are you sure about this one?"

"More than you can imagine." Whatever was broken inside her went quiet when she lay beside Reggie.

And whatever was broken in him, was healed as well.

———

The eyes were wrong.

A study of a thousand artists made painting eyes appear easy. From standard view to molecular macro, every nuance of each painter's technique was revealed. Accessible to recollection.

But technique refused to translate to canvas. Ten scrapings, twenty, five hundred.

And still the eyes were wrong.

4

She had his eyes.

Persephone could only marvel at her daughter. She herself had been named for a hypothetical ninth planet that still had yet to be discovered. Or the goddess of the mythical Greek Underworld, depending on whether she asked Mom or Dad—back when she'd had a Mom and Dad.

She and Reggie had named their daughter Sharon, after Pluto's moon Charon. Charon had also been the boatman of the ferry that delivered the dead across the river Styx into Hades' and Persephone's hands. He might still be out there somewhere shuttling souls across the river.

"We made you," she said in wonder.

Sharon rolled her father-like eyes at her, but there was a smile over her mouthful of chocolate birthday cake.

Persephone had said it every year. Would it be a birthday if she didn't? Or would the moment in her daughter's life pass without meaning if she managed to hold her tongue? This year her words granted her daughter passage over the river of youth and delivered her on the lowest shore of her teens. It was also the year, being of the space-born, that her height would fly past her mother. Persephone was long since resigned to that fate.

Reggie rarely commented. Yet his eyes never strayed from her as she invoked her yearly ritual of uttering the inevitable phrase. It was one of those moments of true inclusion that seemed to exist in only minor facets of his life. Fifteen years together and he still puzzled her. Puzzled, but never disappointed.

He was always the outside observer, but there was no question that the observer witnessed and saw her. Saw their family. In that one tiny sliver, he truly belonged. For without him, there would be no family.

There was no question in her heart when he held her. His merest touch could leave her breathless. She'd often sought evidence of the same effect on his brow, but he was her steadfast pilot through any solar storm.

———

No oil, no canvas could capture her laugh, the light giggle brighter than the stars.

Nothing could fill the void. That darkness.

But something must be created to keep her memory alive.

To hold the candle for a moment.

5

REGGIE KEPT HIS THOUGHTS TO HIMSELF WHEN THE REPORT came in.

Debris.

It had come from behind.

Cerberus' forward repulsion field would have knocked it aside. The side armor would have auto-annealed. It was impossible to know what it had been. The reaction vector said that the debris had been ten kilos moving at seven thousand meters per second relative velocity. It slammed in through the ion drive exhaust nozzle and bullseyed the propellant tank.

One moment his wife and daughter had been entering Mars orbit. He could imagine his daughter's laugh and his wife's giggle. That was the sound he'd most loved as the two of them teased each other. Except for having his eyes and a laugh that was completely her own, their daughter might have been her mother's clone.

Their particle-sized remains had rained down upon

Mars, lost in a dust storm. No memorabilia, only memories.

Unable to deconstruct, he had constructed.

A hand.

It had taken him a year to shape the hand that used to rest so gently upon his cheek that his world went quiet. Over time he'd rebuilt her in her own image.

A foot.

He'd remember how she would sit across a sofa from him, and ever so slowly extend a foot beneath their shared blanket with an ultimate destination of tickling him in the ribs. He'd shaped a foot from that memory.

A leg.

The smooth feel of her calf extending upward as he'd captured it to save his ribs, and then followed it to join their bodies together.

A body.

Reggie had fought against the failures of memory, slowly collecting every vid of her from pilot training to wedding guests to celebrations at the opening of Charon base with her daughter on her hip.

By the time he had her built, his own body was failing. As it reached critical failure, he solved the last step.

He moved his consciousness into the awaiting armature until his hands—were hers.

Android or cyborg. He didn't know. Or care.

The first of his kind. It didn't matter.

His/her new heartbeat felt wrong beneath his new skin, but the sound itself was perfection—a memory from when he used to rest his ear between her breasts every time before they made love.

It had taken decades—many years longer than he'd had her—to achieve this perfect working image.

Without intending, he had become his dead wife.

Yet something was missing.

Something that didn't shine from the new face as he inspected it in the mirror and attempted to bring it to life on the canvas.

But then Reggie saw the reflected eyes.

———

HER FACE.

A hand painting her face. Her hand. Her face.

An ochre overtone highlight for the cheeks.

The onyx fall of her hair always tucked behind the right ear.

The high-grav cheekbone rather than the longer taper of the space-born.

The tip of the nose tugged down by the hint of a smile.

He/she painted his/her own eyes.

They belonged to a machine now.

But these eyes didn't see the snuffing out of the single light in an entire life.

They saw so much more. They saw stars, hope, possibility.

She, the goddess of the Underworld, had always seen the best in him. She had joined their lives together in joy.

Now that he was the perfect image of Persephone, it would be up to him to cross back over the River Styx alone and rediscover the beauty.

He'd finally found her eyes in their painting. In the mirror.

And if he/she was very lucky, perhaps one day he'd rediscover her high, merry laugh.

THE NARA REACTION (EXCERPT)

BERMUDA 2082

"So, I'm dead, am I?"

It was perfect. James Wirden's voice started with all the power one would expect from the World Premier, but it ended the most delicious twist of uncertainty. Bryce looked down at the nearly empty champagne glass in James' hand.

"Yes, sad for you, but true. Poisoned, if you must know. By me."

"And you dare to tell me this?" Such indignation from such a small man. He turned toward the guards, but Bryce clamped a friendly hand upon his shoulder to belay the movement. Not that it mattered, all of the guards along the line of French doors were his hand-picked staff. The bright lights from within cast their tall shadows across the stone terrace pushing back the edge of the Bermudan night. His men would stop any stragglers from the party, not that any would dare interrupt when the Premier and his mighty right-hand man were in conference. But no point in misplacing trust when one staged a coup.

"One of the many things you never properly appreciated, James, is the wonders of modern genetics. There is a tiny little code-alterer running through your system even as we speak. Your genetic code is even now shifting at an exquisitely subtle level. When you have a massive stroke in three days, none shall grieve as much as your lieutenant. None shall take power with as much trepidation as your Right Hand." A nickname Bryce had carefully cultivated for years. Who better to be named to power than the man who knew the Premier's every intent?

The man struggled against his grasp just as pointlessly as a worm evading a short future pithed upon the hook that would send it into the fish's belly. Bryce took the champagne glass from James' nerveless hand and tipped the dregs over the broad stone seawall to splash into the eager waves below. Soon, he promised them, soon you may swallow this useless chattel as well.

The Premier's pale face twisted in such pain that for a moment Bryce feared the stroke would come too soon. He didn't have everything in place yet. Of course, he could compensate, but having the man die in his arms would not look good at all to the World Economic Council.

"You must remember to breathe, my good leader. Besides, in another few minutes you will remember none of this. Another wonder of genetics research you so despise is the revelation of how memories are stored. Your memory of these moments will shortly be erased.

And when you pass on in three day's time, your Right Hand will be there, the Premier-to-be, Bryce Randall Stevens, Sr."

James patted at the beads of sweat on his brow with his small hand as he looked up at Bryce. He always backed up when they spoke so that he didn't have to crane his neck, but Bryce kept him in his place this time. The music surged through the open doors onto the broad patio. The orchestra had come back precisely on schedule drawing everyone's attention inward. He didn't want any to think his conversation with the Premier took overlong if the drug didn't take effect as planned. Of course he knew it would, it had worked perfectly on the man who'd engineered it for him.

"Do you hate me so?"

"Stupid man, what does hate have to do with anything? You're weak, James. Always were. If I hadn't pulled every single string over the last four decades, Parvati and her temple of democratic fairness would still be in power. I have used you, because you are far more presentable than I. No one expects a small, rotund man to be vicious. Therefore, there were no curious eyes as I did what you were too weak to do behind the scenes. But now you are beginning to interfere. You should never have nuked Auckland."

The little man sputtered. "I had to Bryce. You and your damned gene labs. There is a reason we outlawed that horrible knowledge. We did it. You and I. Together. When I found you were dabbling in that dark road to hell, of course I had to blow it out of existence."

"Too little, too late, James. Do you think I'd have let

you drop those bombs if I wasn't ready? All you did for me was a little convenient housecleaning." Actually he'd barely gotten the chief scientists and the data clear. Less than an hour warning had let him salvage only the most essential elements. But the continuing research on the uses of the Second Human Genome Mapping Project lived on, even if the researchers families hadn't. And he'd gotten to look like the hero to the ones he had saved.

The blow of his failure took the fight out of the Premier. Bryce gave James' shoulder a jovial shake in show for any who might be watching.

"On December 24th, three days after this birthday party, lovingly thrown by your second-in-command, I shall mourn at your side. I shall cancel Christmas throughout the planet. It shall be a splendid funeral. And by the New Year, the World Economic Council will place me in command and then things shall really start to move."

James' little eyes squinted up at him for a long moment before turning to look out at the restless sea. He hung onto the rough seawall to keep from being toppled by the gentle night breeze and stared toward the dark waves.

"They will suspect you."

"There will be no proof. The last of the drug has just been dribbled into the sea. The change to your genetic code has already been registered in your electronic medical records, by a fine hacker who has, alas, suffered a memory loss due to some bad fish he ate. Very bad fish. You don't maintain paper files, so I'm safe."

Bryce leaned down to watch his face, but James was

turned toward the night and he was totally in shadow. There was a long hesitation, then a twitch of his shoulders that Bryce could feel beneath his hand.

"But I do. I was most careful."

Not careful enough, old friend. He knew when James' was lying. It was for this that Bryce had risked telling him of his own death. The man was so naive that he hadn't banked hard copies against his future. So, Bryce's plan was going to go off without a hitch.

The Premier hung his head and his voice was a mere whisper against the susurration of the surf on the rocky cliffs below.

"What about my wife?"

Bryce glanced back to the surging dance floor. What an odd final question to ask before certain death. Given a chance, what would be his last request? Not about some woman, that was for certain. Though if ever there was one...

Even through the crowd Celia Wirden stood out. Her fountain of white-blond hair and the slender body beneath, shimmeringly not revealed by her gown of midnight-blue silk, did everything to distract from the brilliant mind that hid behind those green eyes.

The three of them had plotted together since they were young. They had thrown Parvati out of power and when it came time to choose, Bryce had forced the milquetoast James to puppet the Premiership for him. And the Premier needed a First Lady. A fine and elegant First Lady she had made. Perhaps it was time to take that gift back.

"She'll be taken care of, James. You don't need to fear for that."

James' shoulders squared slowly as the man looked a last time at the dark Atlantic. He took up his empty champagne glass from the seawall.

"Well, old friend. Seems that I am dry. Shall we go get a refill?"

"I am right beside you to the end of your days, James."

"Long may that be."

Bryce completed their old code, "Long indeed."

At the French doors, he checked James one last time. But he was filled with a bonhomie that even the finest politician couldn't invent. When he refilled the same glass and drank from it, Bryce knew the memory of the last few minutes was safely gone.

James was wrapped up into the flow of the crowd as Bryce waited upon the threshold. The broad squares of alternating black and white marble spread across the room before him like a grand chess board. The sycophants rushed to make what they could of the moment, shuffling like mad pawns, the tuxedoed livery of the government descended upon the wrong man. The short stature of the largest pawn of them all disappeared from view. Bryce would keep a close eye upon him, but not too close. Nothing must seem out of the ordinary.

He scanned the room. The ladies, those dragged forward by their men, and those abandoned in the sudden rush toward the Premier, glittered about. Their 1920s flapper costumes revealing both the wondrous and the corpulent with an equal lack of sympathy. But they too were all either carefully watching the rush to the Premier, or carefully not watching.

There were just four who were watching the Premier's Right Hand instead. His Captain of the guard, meticulous in his waiter's outfit, was nonchalantly poised to strike from his corner like a steadfast rook. The general commander of the World Economic Council's forces waited like the good knight he was, not obviously aligned, yet always prepared to offer surprise support from unexpected quarters.

Celia Wirden glittered like the queen that she was. The tight silk revealed a mature woman who had grown into her body the way a yacht grows into a World Cup racer. Her movements could light fire without ever striking a match.

His body responded from the memory of that one tryst three decades gone, the same night he'd sent her to become James' first lady. Her green eyes assessed him carefully from her position far across the room near the small orchestra. A chandelier blossomed above her in a font of crystal as if it had bloomed for her alone.

And off to the side, behind the piano, hid a single junior pawn. Without even the boy being aware, Bryce had been moving him across the board, square by careful square. Perhaps it was time to move the lad one step closer to the far side of the board, where he too would become powerful. Together, many things could be achieved. He would kill the king, take the queen, and create a prince.

Yes. It was time for the next move.

Keep reading at fine retailers everywhere.
The Nara Reaction
...and don't forget that review. It really helps me out.

ABOUT THE AUTHOR

M.L. "Matt" Buchman started the first of over 60 novels, 100 short stories, and a fast-growing pile of audiobooks while flying from South Korea to ride his bicycle across the Australian Outback. Part of a solo around the world trip that ultimately launched his writing career in: thrillers, military romantic suspense, contemporary romance, and SF/F.

Recently named in *The 20 Best Romantic Suspense Novels: Modern Masterpieces* by ALA's Booklist, they have also selected his works three times as "Top-10 Romance Novel of the Year." NPR and B&N listed other works as "Best 5 of the Year."

As a 30-year project manager with a geophysics degree who has: designed and built houses, flown and jumped out of planes, and solo-sailed a 50' ketch. He is awed by what's possible. More at: www.mlbuchman.com.

Other works by M. L. Buchman: *(* - also in audio)*

Thrillers

Dead Chef
Swap Out!
One Chef!
Two Chef!

Miranda Chase
*Drone**
*Thunderbolt**

Romantic Suspense

Delta Force
*Target Engaged**
*Heart Strike**
*Wild Justice**
*Midnight Trust**

Firehawks
Main Flight
Pure Heat
Full Blaze
*Hot Point**
*Flash of Fire**
Wild Fire

Smokejumpers
*Wildfire at Dawn**
*Wildfire at Larch Creek**
*Wildfire on the Skagit**

The Night Stalkers
Main Flight
The Night Is Mine
I Own the Dawn
Wait Until Dark
Take Over at Midnight
Light Up the Night
Bring On the Dusk
By Break of Day
and the Navy
Christmas at Steel Beach
Christmas at Peleliu Cove

White House Holiday
*Daniel's Christmas**
*Frank's Independence Day**
*Peter's Christmas**
*Zachary's Christmas**
*Roy's Independence Day**
*Damien's Christmas**
5E
Target of the Heart
Target Lock on Love
Target of Mine
Target of One's Own

Shadow Force: Psi
*At the Slightest Sound**
*At the Quietest Word**

White House Protection Force
*Off the Leash**
*On Your Mark**
*In the Weeds**

Contemporary Romance

Eagle Cove
Return to Eagle Cove
Recipe for Eagle Cove
Longing for Eagle Cove
Keepsake for Eagle Cove

Henderson's Ranch
*Nathan's Big Sky**
*Big Sky, Loyal Heart**
*Big Sky Dog Whisperer**

Love Abroad
Heart of the Cotswolds: England
Path of Love: Cinque Terre, Italy

Other works by M. L. Buchman:

Contemporary Romance (cont)

Where Dreams
Where Dreams are Born
Where Dreams Reside
Where Dreams Are of Christmas
Where Dreams Unfold
Where Dreams Are Written

Science Fiction / Fantasy

Deities Anonymous
Cookbook from Hell: Reheated
Saviors 101

Single Titles
The Nara Reaction
Monk's Maze
the Me and Elsie Chronicles

Non-Fiction

Strategies for Success
Managing Your Inner Artist/Writer
*Estate Planning for Authors**
Character Voice
*Narrate and Record Your Own Audiobook**

Short Story Series by M. L. Buchman:

Romantic Suspense

Delta Force
Delta Force

Firehawks
The Firehawks Lookouts
The Firehawks Hotshots
The Firebirds

The Night Stalkers
The Night Stalkers
The Night Stalkers 5E
The Night Stalkers CSAR
The Night Stalkers Wedding Stories

US Coast Guard
US Coast Guard

White House Protection Force
White House Protection Force

Contemporary Romance

Eagle Cove
Eagle Cove

Henderson's Ranch
Henderson's Ranch

Where Dreams
Where Dreams

Thrillers

Dead Chef
Dead Chef

Science Fiction / Fantasy

Deities Anonymous
Deities Anonymous

Other
The Future Night Stalkers
Single Titles

SIGN UP FOR M. L. BUCHMAN'S NEWSLETTER TODAY

and receive:
Release News
Free Short Stories
a Free Book

Get your free book today. Do it now.
free-book.mlbuchman.com